The Donkey's First christmas

susanne T schroder

For my Dad's friends
& West Kirby URC
(Thank you)

tilli Publishing

www.tillipublishing.com

The Donkey's First Christmas
ISBN 978-1-908053-02-2
First Published 2011
This Edition Published 2015

Tilli Publishing Ltd is Registered in the UK No 07702060

Printed in London, England.

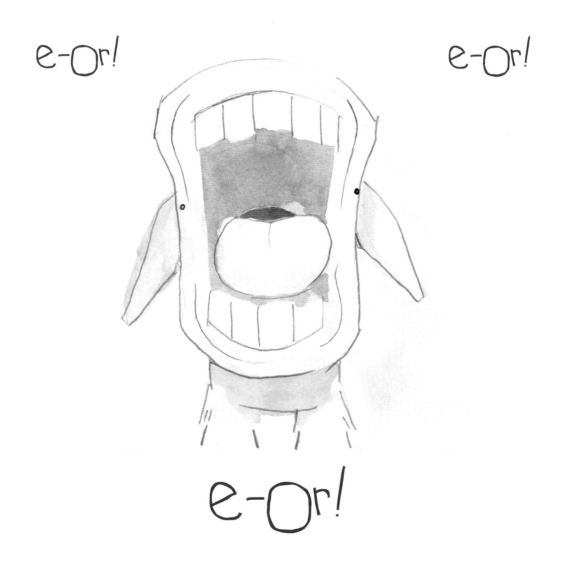

Funny little donkey
standing in the yard.
Tell us why you're braying
so very

very

loud?

I bray to tell
the story
Of a very
precious
load

I once was asked
to carry
down a long and
dusty road.

My owner called me useless

I drove him quite berserk

Because I'd find all <u>kinds</u> of ways

to get out of my work.

I might try looking ill...

or hide behind some hay

so passers-by would hire a
different donkey
for the day.

This one time though,
a man turned up

Who would not be put off...
Even though I hid...

and limped...

and eeyored
l o u d...

and
coughed!

"I'll take him now" the young man said.

"Just tell me, What's your fee?"

My desperate owner laughed amazed,

"Just take him -he's for free!"

My heart sank
      as I left the yard
and saw my load to bear...

A woman with a

         massive bump

and bags,

      was standing there.

"I won't and you can't make me help!"
I challenged with a stare...
But then, instead of scolding me,
she just produced a pear!

"There you go - you sweetie
let's have a bite to eat

(It wouldn't do to start our trip
without a little treat) "

"Oh well, I guess I'll help a bit
- but only for today!

And so, I plodded onward
until I heard her say:

"You clever little donkey –
just look how far we've come!

If not for all this help from you,

what would we all have done?"

I felt my posture straighten,
and strength come to my knees,
My plodding slow pace quickened,
to make the woman pleased.

Then every time she woke up
she would tell me once again,
  "Thank you, faithful donkey"
as she rested on my mane.

At last I'd reached my limit

    – couldn't take another step!

But then, I heard
    my lady's cry

and saw her start
    to fret...

"I feel the baby's coming

        - He's ready to be born!"

So though
I felt
exhausted,

my hooves
all scratched
and torn,

I pulled myself together,
and used up all my might
To take the lady further,
to the nearest town in sight.

Then when we reached the shelter
and I knew that she was safe,
I fell down on the stable floor
– fell flat upon my face!

The next thing I remember
was the unfamiliar sound...

...Of a little baby crying
from a manger, on the ground.

Then when I saw the mother
pull her tiny baby near,
An angel who'd been watching
leant and whispered in my ear,

"You see now little donkey
-what a special

thing you've

done?

By helping carry Mary,
you helped

God's precious

son."